To my brothers,
John and Tim

Henry Holt and Company, LLC
Publishers since 1866
175 Fifth Avenue
New York, New York 10010
www.henryholtchildrensbooks.com

Library of Congress Cataloging-in-Publication Data
McCarty, Peter.
Fabian escapes / written and illustrated by Peter McCarty.—1st ed.
p.   cm.
Summary: While Hondo the dog stays home and enjoys his usual pursuits,
Fabian the cat escapes out the window and has many adventures.
ISBN-13: 978-0-8050-7713-1 / ISBN-10: 0-8050-7713-8
[1. Cats—Fiction. 2. Dogs—Fiction. 3. Adventure and adventurers.] I. Title.
PZ7.M12835Fab 2007   [E]—dc22   2006030614

First Edition—2007
The artist used pencil on watercolor paper to create the illustrations for this book.
Printed in China on acid-free paper. ∞
1 3 5 7 9 10 8 6 4 2

Fabian Escapes

written and illustrated by

Peter McCarty

Henry Holt and Company
New York

Fabian on the windowsill,
Hondo on the floor—
two sleepy pets
in their favorite places.

"Wake up, Hondo.
Let's go for a walk!"

Hondo comes in after his walk
around the block.
Hondo will stay home.

Fabian escapes out the window.

Fabian will have an adventure.

Fabian strolls through the garden.
He stops to smell the flowers
and eats them.

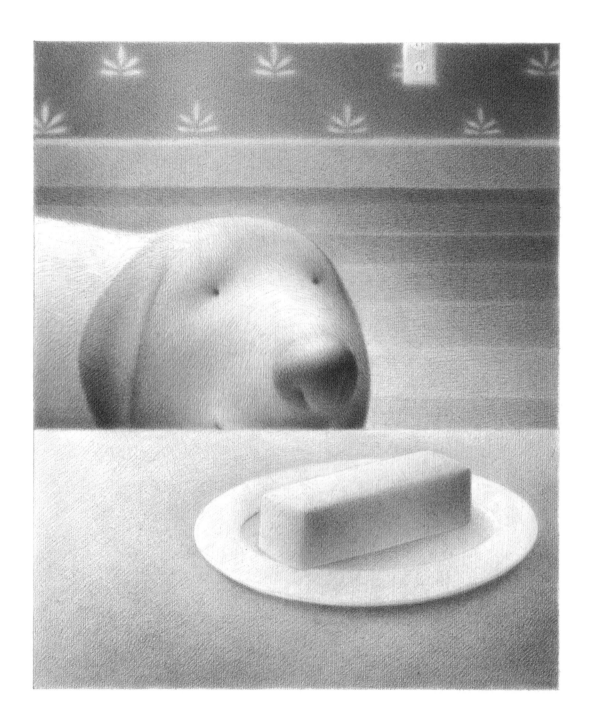

Hondo goes to the kitchen.
He stops to smell the butter
and eats it.

Fabian walks across the yard.

He meets the neighbors.

Hondo walks across the room.

He gets a cracker from the baby.

The neighbors are happy
to play chase with their new friend.

The baby is happy
to play dress-up with Hondo.

Fabian leaps over a fence.

Hondo sneaks upstairs.

Fabian spends the rest of the day hiding under the porch.

Hondo spends the rest of the day napping on the bed.

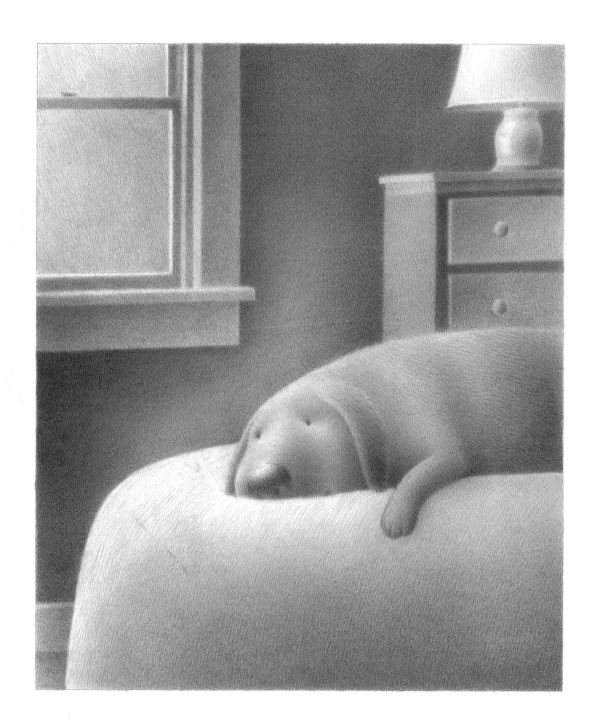

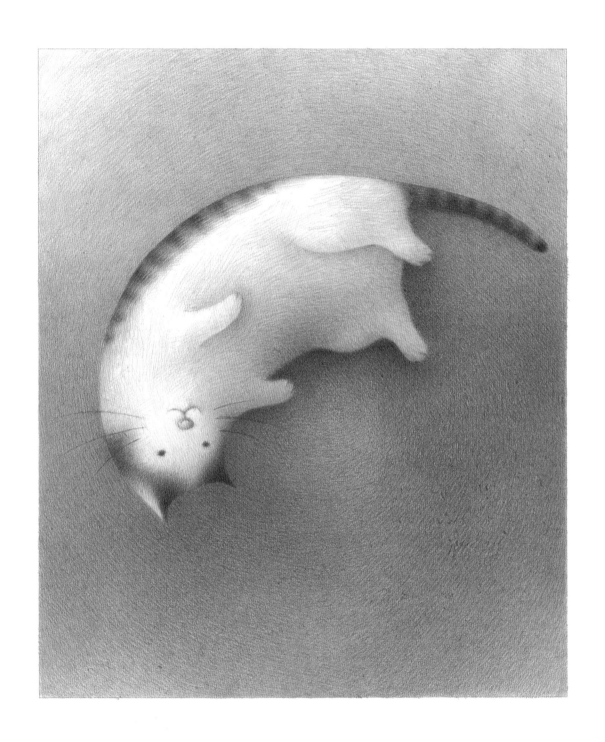

Fabian rolls in the dirt.

He hears the front door open.

Hondo goes out for another walk.
Fabian dives back inside.

"Where have you been, Fabian?"

"Welcome home!"

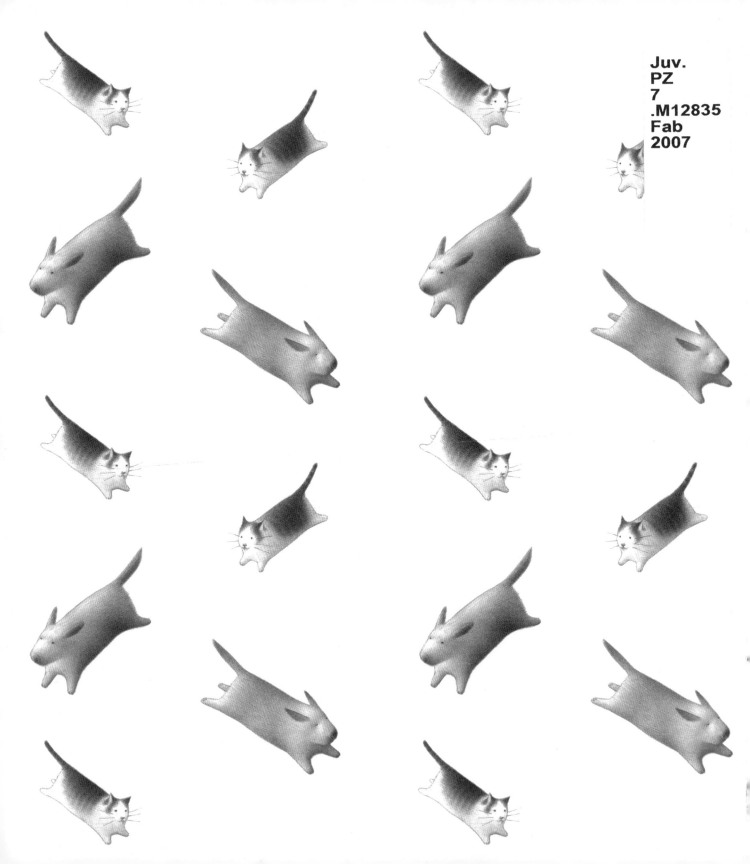